Beast Quest

A to Z of Beasts

ORCHARD BOOKS
Carmelite House
50 Victoria Embankment
London EC4Y 0DZ

Beast Quest is a registered trademark of Beast Quest Limited
Series created by Beast Quest Limited, London

First published in 2015
This edition Published in 2016 by The Watts Publishing Group.
Text © Beast Quest Limited 2015
Cover illustrations: Arcta, Ferno and Tagus © David Wyatt 2007. All others ©
Orchard Books 2007-2015
Inside illustrations: Arcta, Epos, Ferno, Nanook, Sepron and Tagus © David Wyatt
2007. Arachnid, Claw, Soltra, Trillion, Vedra & Krimon, Vipero and Zepha ©
David Wyatt 2008
All other inside illustrations © Beast Quest Limited 2007-2015

A CIP catalogue record for this book is available from the British Library.

ISBN 978 1 40833 839 1

Printed in China

MIX
Paper from
responsible sources
FSC® C104740

The paper and board used in this book are made from wood
from responsible sources.

Orchard Books
An imprint of Hachette Children's Group
Part of The Watts Publishing Group Limited
An Hachette UK Company

www.hachette.co.uk
www.beastquest.co.uk

Beast Quest

A to Z of Beasts

ORCHARD

CONTENTS

WELCOME TO AVANTIA!

IN THIS BOOK YOU'LL FIND FACTS,
STATISTICS AND FASCINATING
STORIES ABOUT ALL THE BEASTS TOM
HAS TACKLED ON HIS BEAST QUESTS.

READ ON AND YOU TOO
COULD BECOME

MASTER OF THE BEASTS!

ADURO

Wise old Aduro has long served King Hugo as the Wizard of Avantia. He is Tom's guide on his Beast Quests – his knowledge of Avantia's history and terrain, as well as the Beasts' weaknesses, has proved life-saving on many occasions.

7

GOOD

AGE	70
POWER	276
MAGIC LEVEL	192
FRIGHT FACTOR	65
SIZE	50

ALDROIM
THE SHAPE-SHIFTER

EVIL

Aldroim dwells in the network of secret tunnels that lie deep beneath Avantia. He is a four-legged, cat-like Beast, with eyes like burning coals and razor-sharp talons that can cut through rock. Aldroim's skin is made up of the feathers, scales, broken bones and hides of his victims.

8

0	AGE
234	POWER
179	MAGIC LEVEL
82	FRIGHT FACTOR
207	SIZE

AMICTUS

THE BUG QUEEN

Ancient scrolls found in Gwildor tell us that Amictus lays beautiful, shimmering eggs on the jungle floor. A highly protective mother, she guards her young fiercely, but will only attack with her poisoned claws and spiky limbs as a last resort.

GOOD

AGE	288
POWER	199
MAGIC LEVEL	189
FRIGHT FACTOR	92
SIZE	291

ANORET
THE FIRST BEAST

It is believed that this lizard-like creature was the very first to rampage through the kingdom of Avantia. Long ago a warlord stole the Beast's face and wore it as a mask – the "Mask of Death" – giving himself the power to control Anoret.

10

DANGER DESTINY

Read Anoret's story in Beast Quest Special 12!

GOOD

A

Hundreds of years after this epic battle, Kensa the Witch sought to use the Mask to control not only the First Beast, but six young and innocent Beasts as well.

11

AGE	500+
POWER	296
MAGIC LEVEL	195
FRIGHT FACTOR	98
SIZE	460

ARACHNID

THE KING OF SPIDERS

Arachnid lurks in caves near the village of Spindrel, in southern Avantia. He is a giant spider, capable of catching grown men in his webs and consuming them.

EVIL

285 AGE
156 POWER
142 MAGIC LEVEL
78 FRIGHT FACTOR
255 SIZE

ARAX

THE SOUL STEALER

Arax was found in a cave in the mountain range of southwest Avantia. The Beast uses a long whip to snare his victims and steal their souls.

EVIL

AGE	271
POWER	242
MAGIC LEVEL	187
FRIGHT FACTOR	92
SIZE	125

ARCTA
THE MOUNTAIN GIANT

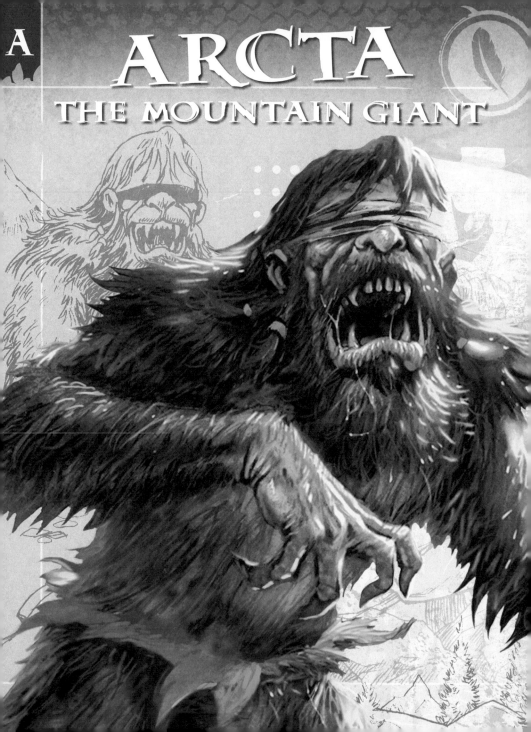

GOOD

Arcta is the last Cyclops of the Northern Mountains. These Beasts once dwelt at the top of the highest peaks, and protected the other mountain creatures. Like all Cyclopes, Arcta has only one eye. He is as tall as the pine forests that grow across the mountain slopes, with claws that can tear into chunks of rock.

15

DANGER · DESTINY

Arcta gave Tom a magical feather, which allows him to float through the air.

AGE	324
POWER	132
MAGIC LEVEL	120
FRIGHT FACTOR	65
SIZE	480

B BALISK
THE WATER SNAKE

O ne of the Beasts conjured by Sanpao the Pirate King, Balisk lurks in the Western Ocean. His long, powerful body is covered in tough scales and his fins have sharp claws. Dagger-sharp fangs fill his gaping mouth.

16

DANGER DESTINY

Tom used one of Balisk's claws like a boomerang.

EVIL

278	AGE
237	POWER
171	MAGIC LEVEL
90	FRIGHT FACTOR
333	SIZE

BLAZE
THE ICE DRAGON

DANGER · DESTINY

Tom used his own shadow to defeat Blaze!

EVIL

Many hundreds of years ago, the whole of Avantia was covered in a sheet of ice. The Great Thaw restored life to the land, but for some parts of the realm, Blaze the Ice Dragon has unleashed a second Ice Age. Most dragons breathe fire, but from Blaze's jaws blasts a deadly stream of icy wind. The Beast freezes everything in his path – water, animals and plants. Nothing can escape.

AGE	313
POWER	210
MAGIC LEVEL	187
FRIGHT FACTOR	90
SIZE	320

BLOODBOAR
THE BURIED DOOM

Bloodboar is covered in plates of thick warty hide as tough as any armour. The size of a barn, he towers over people but moves surprisingly quickly on short, powerful legs. If you're not crushed beneath his pounding hooves, you'll have to contend with his jutting yellow tusks. They're strong enough to rip houses to pieces with a shake of the Beast's head.

20

233	AGE
350	POWER
180	MAGIC LEVEL
86	FRIGHT FACTOR
140	SIZE

21

Tom used a fragment of Bloodboar's armour as a deadly throwing star.

DANGER DESTINY

BRUTUS

THE HOUND OF HORROR

Brutus is a giant dog who hides in the fog of the marshlands of Henkrall. Some say he can actually turn into fog to evade capture or sneak up on his victims. He hovers in the air on huge leathery wings, which waft a suffocating stink. Brutus was made by the sorceress Kensa using the blood of Epos the Flame Bird.

22

0	AGE
285	POWER
189	MAGIC LEVEL
90	FRIGHT FACTOR
244	SIZE

EVIL

B

23

DANGER · DESTINY

In Henkrall,
all the Beasts
and people
can fly!

C

CARNIVORA
THE WINGED SCAVENGER

Carnivora is like a hyena but much larger, with jagged teeth and wicked yellow eyes that seem to ooze pus. Even on land she would be terrifying, but she can also fly! Carnivora's most lethal weapon is her fiery breath.

GOOD

24

293	AGE
250	POWER
180	MAGIC LEVEL
86	FRIGHT FACTOR
262	SIZE

25

DANGER ⌇⌇ DESTINY

Carnivora can melt frozen lakes, making even the landscape deadly!

CLAW

THE GIANT MONKEY

Claw roams Avantia's Dark Jungle – a place where few dare to venture, and fewer still return alive. His chest is as wide as a horse is long, and his arms are thicker than most of the trees in the jungle. His eyes are a frightening shade of yellow, and he has gigantic clawed hands. But his deadliest weapon is his long tail, which ends in an extra claw.

EVIL

465	AGE
217	POWER
134	MAGIC LEVEL
68	FRIGHT FACTOR
200	SIZE

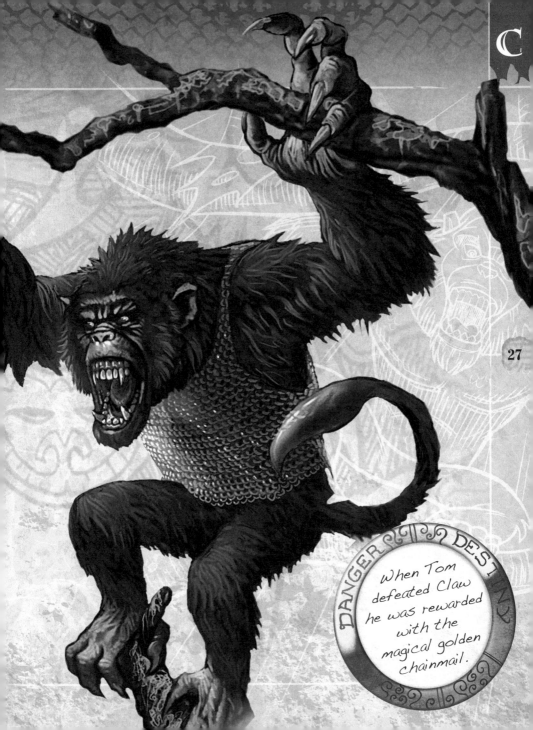

27

When Tom defeated Claw he was rewarded with the magical golden chainmail.

CONVOL

THE COLD-BLOODED BRUTE

Convol is the largest desert lizard in the known realms. His back and tail are covered with ferocious spikes and his thick, scaly skin is almost impenetrable. His rotten teeth glisten in the desert sun, his body is covered with revolting warts and his gums are a sickening green.

300	AGE
230	POWER
171	MAGIC LEVEL
81	FRIGHT FACTOR
244	SIZE

GOOD

CORNIX

THE DEADLY TRICKSTER

At first, Cornix seems to be a beautiful woman with long dark hair, wrapped in a cloak of red velvet and carrying a lantern. But beneath her cloak is the rotting, feathered body of a crow. Her bird-like feet have vicious claws, and her face is a gruesome human skull. Cornix conjures strange lights to lure travellers. She then envelops them in her cloak – and consumes them.

EVIL

29

AGE	0
POWER	209
MAGIC LEVEL	188
FRIGHT FACTOR	81
SIZE	104

CRETA

THE WINGED TERROR

This Beast is made of countless flying insects forming a column, which then sprouts arms and wings. Creta has terrifying fangs and two mighty horns.

227	AGE
281	POWER
170	MAGIC LEVEL
90	FRIGHT FACTOR
290	SIZE

D altec is a young wizard. Formerly Aduro's apprentice, he now aids Tom and Elenna on their Quests.

GOOD

AGE	21
POWER	252
MAGIC LEVEL	189
FRIGHT FACTOR	49
SIZE	50

DOOMSKULL

THE KING OF FEAR

Doomskull's most unnerving features are his eye sockets, which are completely empty. The Beast invades the nightmares of all who are unfortunate enough to gaze upon him. He looks like a lion made of stone, but up close, his victims can see his rippling muscles and sabre-tooth fangs.

EVIL

339	AGE
222	POWER
141	MAGIC LEVEL
83	FRIGHT FACTOR
150	SIZE

D

33

Tom became
Master of
the Beasts
after defeating
Doomskull!

DANGER DESTINY

DREDDA

THE TUNNELLING MENACE

Dredda's body is like a giant snake, and her diamond-tipped claws are deadly. Her teeth are powerful enough to chomp through stone and turn it to dust. Tom found a way to get the better of her by targeting the tiny patch of weak flesh on the underside of her jaw. Only a true hero of Avantia could tackle this Beast!

34

EVIL

3	AGE
264	POWER
148	MAGIC LEVEL
88	FRIGHT FACTOR
233	SIZE

ELENNA

Elenna is an expert archer whose arrows always strike true. She was brought up by her uncle Leo, a fisherman, after her parents died in a fire. Elenna has been by Tom's side since his first Beast Quest and is a loyal friend and brave fighter.

35

GOOD

AGE	12
POWER	56
MAGIC LEVEL	91
FRIGHT FACTOR	68
SIZE	38

ELKO
THE OCEAN MENACE

Elko's mouth is lined with deadly fangs, and his hideous limbs can regenerate when severed by a blade. Elko was created by Kensa to wreak havoc on the kingdom of Henkrall.

EVIL

0	AGE
286	POWER
188	MAGIC LEVEL
91	FRIGHT FACTOR
287	SIZE

ELLIK

THE LIGHTNING HORROR

Ellik lurks in swampy water where she can remain hidden from her prey. Despite her thick body she can dart in the blink of an eye to snatch victims in her sharp fangs. Ellik's blue scales suck lightning from the sky and she stores the charge, ready to give her enemies a nasty shock!

GOOD

AGE	287
POWER	247
MAGIC LEVEL	177
FRIGHT FACTOR	85
SIZE	380

EPOS
THE FLAME BIRD

Epos, known to some as the Flame Bird, is one of the oldest Beasts in the Kingdom of Avantia. She is a phoenix who fears no injury or attack, because she can heal herself with fiery magic. Nobody knows exactly how many times this Beast has been reborn in the molten depths of the Stonewin Volcano, but while she guards it, the kingdom is safe from disaster.

GOOD

457	AGE
243	POWER
192	MAGIC LEVEL
92	FRIGHT FACTOR
240	SIZE

DANGER · DESTINY

One of Tom's treasures is the healing talon given to him by Epos.

EQUINUS
THE SPIRIT HORSE

O ne of the most vile and dangerous of the Ghost-Beasts who dwell in the Forbidden Land is Equinus the Spirit Horse. His skeletal face is a mask of hatred and evil, frightening all wildlife in the Dead Jungle, where he has made his lair. When Equinus is in his ghostly form, it is possible to see the Beast's black heart.

40

EVIL

310	AGE
189	POWER
181	MAGIC LEVEL
85	FRIGHT FACTOR
148	SIZE

FALRA
THE SNOW PHOENIX

This young white phoenix grew up in Rion, under the watchful eye of the Beast-Keeper Wilfred. Her wings ripple with flames, and her talons drip lava, but Falra is a sworn defender of Good now that Tom has freed her from Kensa's dark magic.

41

GOOD

AGE	6
POWER	240
MAGIC LEVEL	155
FRIGHT FACTOR	86
SIZE	237

F

FANG
THE BAT FIEND

EVIL

265	AGE
253	POWER
172	MAGIC LEVEL
77	FRIGHT FACTOR
266	SIZE

Fang lives in underground caves at the bottom of the Golden Valley of Kayonia. A giant bat with leathery wings like sails, Fang has dagger-sharp teeth and grasping claws which make him a deadly predator. When he's not in flight, Fang is almost impossible to spot in the darkness, but if you get too close to him you'll go blind!

DANGER DESTINY

Tom and Elenna defeated Fang on their Quest to help save Tom's mother, Freya.

FERNO
THE FIRE DRAGON

In caves in the south, by Avantia's Winding River, lurks Ferno the Fire Dragon. Ferno is so enormous, he has been mistaken for one of the mountains. The Fire Dragon patrols the river and makes sure that the southern towns of the kingdom are never flooded. Should the waters rise, he can use his clawed feet to build protective dams. Their sudden appearances confuse the locals – but they are very grateful for them!

44

GOOD

288	AGE
212	POWER
180	MAGIC LEVEL
91	FRIGHT FACTOR
465	SIZE

F

Ferno
gave Tom
a magical
dragon scale
for his
shield.

DANGER DESTINY

FERROK

THE IRON SOLDIER

This giant is formed from molten iron, and uses his sharp sword to magically draw flame into his body and increase his strength. The sword is not his only mode of attack – when Tom challenged the Beast, Ferrok conjured a net of fiery ropes to keep him subdued. The battle was one of Tom's deadliest ever!

46

DANGER **DESTINY**

Ferrok can enchant people and turn them into his servants.

217	AGE
293	POWER
180	MAGIC LEVEL
94	FRIGHT FACTOR
151	SIZE

47

FLAYMAR
THE SCORCHING BLAZE

This terrifying monster is a Beast made of molten rock and flame, created in the image of the evil sorceress Kensa. Flaymar uses a whip of fire to attack her enemies and torment the people of Henkrall, and can turn herself into lava.

EVIL

0	AGE
293	POWER
190	MAGIC LEVEL
91	FRIGHT FACTOR
122	SIZE

FREYA

GOOD

F

A s deadly as she is beautiful, Freya first appeared as the evil wizard Velmal's companion. But it turned out that this mysterious woman was actually Tom's long-lost mother!

AGE	44
POWER	190
MAGIC LEVEL	170
FRIGHT FACTOR	78
SIZE	51

G

GRASHKOR
THE BEAST GUARD

Grashkor was an Evil Beast who killed a former Master of the Beasts. As a punishment he was sent by the Wizard Aduro to the Chamber of Pain, an island prison that floats in the stormy seas of the Western Ocean. There he guards the inmates, swooping over the battlements on leathery wings, and cracking his bone whip.

257	AGE
289	POWER
150	MAGIC LEVEL
90	FRIGHT FACTOR
280	SIZE

DANGER · DESTINY

Look out for Grashkor in Series 15, when Tom and Elenna travel to Tangala...

EVIL

H

HAWKITE

ARROW OF THE AIR

Hawkite is an immense, fiery bird with glowing red eyes and razor-sharp talons. She is an agile flyer and can outmanoeuvre anyone who tries to attack Gwildor. Hawkite protects the land and its people.

GOOD

457	AGE
211	POWER
159	MAGIC LEVEL
89	FRIGHT FACTOR
260	SIZE

HECTON

THE BODY SNATCHER

Hecton is tall and bony with skin the colour of rotting flesh. He wears a cloak sewn together from scraps of fur and feathers, and a bull's head as a hood. He uses a net and a trident to trap his victims.

53

AGE	302
POWER	294
MAGIC LEVEL	188
FRIGHT FACTOR	96
SIZE	101

HELLION
THE FIERY FOE

This Beast's lair is deep in an active volcano. His body is like a column of flame, as tall as a blazing house. If he senses a threat, Hellion curls into a ball and rolls across the ground like a hurtling bonfire, scorching everything in his path.

297	AGE
235	POWER
159	MAGIC LEVEL
82	FRIGHT FACTOR
132	SIZE

KING HUGO

Good King Hugo never planned to sit on Avantia's throne, but when his older brother died in battle, he was left with no choice. A kindly monarch who is loved by his people, he sent Tom on his first ever Beast Quest and Tom has served him loyally ever since.

55

GOOD

AGE	56
POWER	243
MAGIC LEVEL	40
FRIGHT FACTOR	70
SIZE	55

ISSRILLA
THE CREEPING MENACE

Issrilla is a mistress of disguise. This lizard Beast from the kingdom of Henkrall can blend into any background. Her skeleton is covered in jelly-flesh that changes colour, and she can sneak up on her enemies without being detected.

I

56

EVIL

DANGER • DESTIN

Issrilla spits deadly acid venom that can burn flesh.

I

AGE	340
POWER	262
MAGIC LEVEL	193
FRIGHT FACTOR	93
SIZE	305

JAKARA
THE GHOST WARRIOR

Jakara is perhaps the most tragic Beast Tom has encountered. She is a hideous, magical fusion of the Ghost Beast Jalka and Kara, a former Mistress of the Beasts. When Aduro set off on his own Quest to find Kara, Tom followed.

58

DANGER DESTINY

Kara now rests in peace in the Gallery of Tombs.

60	AGE
296	POWER
185	MAGIC LEVEL
89	FRIGHT FACTOR
55	SIZE

He was faced with the task of finding a way to free the Good Warrior from the awful fate of being bound to an Evil Beast for ever…

59

KAJIN
THE BEAST CATCHER

This Beast towers on two legs like a man, but has the body of a wolf, covered in a shaggy pelt. Under a snarling snout, sabre-like teeth can rip his prey to shreds. Kajin uses his powerful net to capture Beasts and people alike.

60

EVIL

399	AGE
243	POWER
152	MAGIC LEVEL
87	FRIGHT FACTOR
288	SIZE

K

There's no escape from the strands of Kajin's net!

DANGER • DESTINY

KAMA
THE FACELESS BEAST

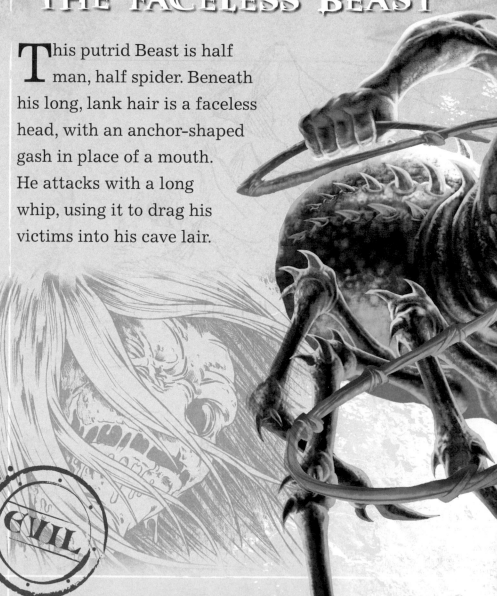

This putrid Beast is half man, half spider. Beneath his long, lank hair is a faceless head, with an anchor-shaped gash in place of a mouth. He attacks with a long whip, using it to drag his victims into his cave lair.

EVIL

K

63

Kama has just one evil black eye.

DANGER DEST

AGE 419
POWER 254
MAGIC LEVEL 146
FRIGHT FACTOR 92
SIZE 105

KAYMON
THE GORGON HOUND

This gigantic dog can split her body for multiple deadly attacks. Kaymon lurks among the ruins of an ancient Gorgonian castle. Her huge paws can crush the bones of even the strongest warrior, and her massive jaws can swallow children whole. Avantia is lucky that this Beast has not yet found a way into the kingdom.

64

DANGER DESTINY

Kaymon held Nanook the Snow Monster captive.

EVIL

K

65

AGE 296
POWER 239
MAGIC LEVEL 157
FRIGHT FACTOR 85
SIZE 152

KLAXA

THE ARMOURED ENEMY

 Klaxa is twice as large as a rhinoceros. Many a warrior has been fooled into underestimating her as little more than a lumbering Beast. But Klaxa is cunning – she can retract her legs and head into her body so that, from a distance, she looks like a boulder. Then, when people wander past, she reveals herself and uses her poisonous horn to impale her victims.

232	AGE
210	POWER
179	MAGIC LEVEL
82	FRIGHT FACTOR
251	SIZE

EVIL

67

DANGER · DESTINY

This Beast's hide is incredibly tough!

KOBA
GHOUL OF THE SHADOWS

At the end of The Warrior's Road Tom encountered this terrifying shape-shifter. His true form is of a muscular, genie-like Beast with huge clawed hands – but this ghoul delights in changing into other forms, to weaken the resolve of heroes and adventurers who cross his path.

68

EVIL

400	AGE
280	POWER
184	MAGIC LEVEL
93	FRIGHT FACTOR
140	SIZE

DANGER DESTINY

Koba's green eye became a powerful token of evil magic.

KOLDO

THE ARCTIC WARRIOR

This spiky Beast is a giant made of ice. Despite his strength, Koldo is gentle – unless provoked by an enemy of Gwildor. There are rumours that the people of the kingdom have tried to capture Koldo, though it is difficult to believe anyone would be so foolhardy.

GOOD

70

335	AGE
183	POWER
166	MAGIC LEVEL
84	FRIGHT FACTOR
115	SIZE

71

DANGER · DESTINY

When Koldo was set free from Velmal's curse he helped rescue Tom.

KOMODO
THE LIZARD KING

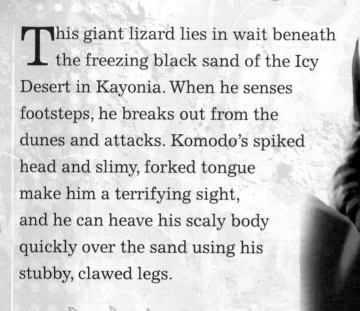

This giant lizard lies in wait beneath the freezing black sand of the Icy Desert in Kayonia. When he senses footsteps, he breaks out from the dunes and attacks. Komodo's spiked head and slimy, forked tongue make him a terrifying sight, and he can heave his scaly body quickly over the sand using his stubby, clawed legs.

DANGER • DESTINY

Komodo has a hide as thick as chainmail.

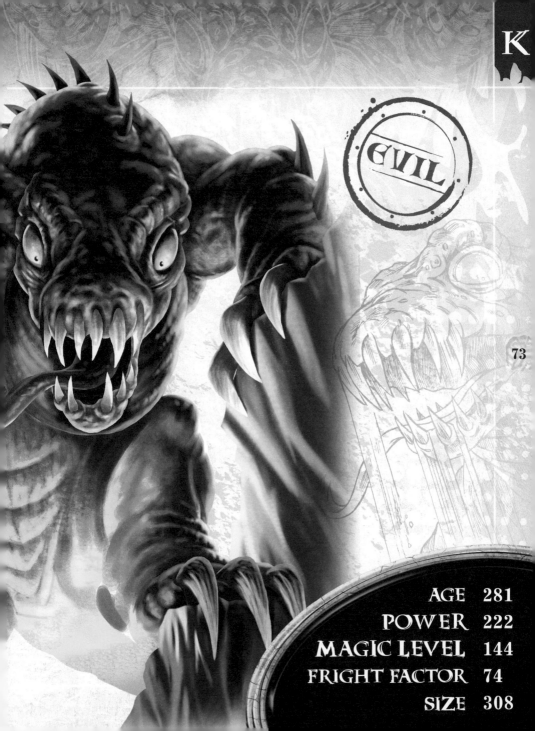

EVIL

73

AGE 281
POWER 222
MAGIC LEVEL 144
FRIGHT FACTOR 74
SIZE 308

KORAKA

THE WINGED ASSASSIN

With her scaly legs, huge wings and fearsome talons, it would be easy to dismiss Koraka as a lumbering animal. But she is clever enough to carry a spear as well, giving her several options for attack. Koraka was once a good, innocent shepherdess, but the witch Petra used her magic to turn Koraka evil.

74

DANGER DESTINY

Tom defeated Koraka with help from flocks of birds.

25	AGE
260	POWER
167	MAGIC LEVEL
93	FRIGHT FACTOR
101	SIZE

75

KORON
JAWS OF DEATH

This Beast is well named: hidden behind his black lips are teeth like daggers. Koron's muscular body is like a tiger's, and claws as sharp as the deadliest blade will tear your head from your shoulders. Most terrifying of all, he has a scorpion's tail that can dart forward as fast as a whip to attack his victims.

389	AGE
270	POWER
167	MAGIC LEVEL
94	FRIGHT FACTOR
119	SIZE

EVIL

DANGER! DESTINY

Koron's fangs drip a burning spittle that nearly destroyed Tom's shield!

KRABB
MASTER OF THE SEA

Krabb dwells in the ocean to the east of Gwildor. With a huge shell bristling with bony spikes, and six stabbing legs, Krabb protects the creatures of the sea. His armoured underbelly provides a home for many colonies of barnacles, and sea anemones cluster along his spiny back.

261	AGE
190	POWER
184	MAGIC LEVEL
88	FRIGHT FACTOR
277	SIZE

GOOD

79

Krabb saves food from his meals for his passengers.

KRAGOS AND KILDOR
THE TWO-HEADED DEMON

This two-headed Beast can change and re-form itself into different creatures. It last appeared in the form of a ram and a stag. The Two-Headed Demon desires the magical golden Cup of Life, a precious object which will protect anyone who drinks from it against death.

302	AGE
282	POWER
191	MAGIC LEVEL
91	FRIGHT FACTOR
140	SIZE

EVIL

DANGER DESTINY

The Cup of
Life must be
kept in fire to
preserve its
magic.

KRESTOR

THE CRUSHING TERROR

This Beast has the neck of a serpent, coated in green scales, with powerful legs and webbed claws that propel him through the water. Krestor's red eyes can search out prey in the gloomiest depths. The Beast's snaking coils can squeeze the life out of his victims. His other deadly weapons are the jagged spines along his back. They can shoot acid strong enough to melt flesh and bone.

82

DANGER DESTINY

Krestor's thick scales were too tough for Elenna's arrows.

313	AGE
240	POWER
167	MAGIC LEVEL
83	FRIGHT FACTOR
373	SIZE

EVIL

KRONUS

THE CLAWED MENACE

An enormous vulture, this Beast's oily wings give out a dreadful stench and its beak opens wider than the tallest man. Beams of blinding red light burst from its glowing eyes, powerful enough to cut through stone. Its great claws can tear a person's throat out.

85

DANGER DESTINY

Nanook the Snow Monster helped to defeat Kronus.

EVIL

AGE	313
POWER	280
MAGIC LEVEL	191
FRIGHT FACTOR	98
SIZE	307

UNCLE LEO

The fisherman who raised Elenna after her parents' death, Leo is a kind and honourable man, always ready to offer his niece and her best friend whatever support he can.

GOOD

54 AGE
74 POWER
20 MAGIC LEVEL
18 FRIGHT FACTOR
46 SIZE

LINKA

THE SKY CONQUEROR

EVIL

At a distance, Linka might be mistaken for a sort of eagle, with her tawny feathers. But the Beast has no talons, or even feet. Her lower half is a feathered tail, covered in thick scales and ending in a stinger. By the time her victims can hear her shriek, it's too late for them.

AGE	390
POWER	249
MAGIC LEVEL	131
FRIGHT FACTOR	92
SIZE	250

LUNA

THE MOON WOLF

In the Forbidden Land's Dark Wood lurks Luna the Moon Wolf. Her claws are sharper than the deadliest of daggers, and her teeth can tear holes in any armour. But her most powerful and dangerous weapon is her ability to exert control over animals unlucky enough to be nearby.

DANGER DESTINY

Luna's cubs are as vicious as their mother!

L

EVIL

89

AGE	257
POWER	209
MAGIC LEVEL	183
FRIGHT FACTOR	84
SIZE	132

LUSTOR

THE ACID DART

From his hiding place among the moss and rocks, Lustor emerges to reveal a toad-like face covered in warts. He has eyes like a fish and a long, curling tongue. Beneath his throat is a sac filled with a bright orange liquid that sprays in jets, burning through flesh.

90

328	AGE
235	POWER
159	MAGIC LEVEL
85	FRIGHT FACTOR
247	SIZE

MADARA
THE MIDNIGHT WARRIOR

Madara is a giant cat who stalks the chilly mountains in the north of Tavania. Against the snow, she's almost invisible because of her crystal-white fur, and her lidless yellow eyes are always on the lookout for prey or danger.

GOOD

AGE	290
POWER	245
MAGIC LEVEL	173
FRIGHT FACTOR	84
SIZE	256

AUNT MARIA AND UNCLE HENRY

Tom was brought up by his uncle and aunt in the village of Errinel, where Uncle Henry is a blacksmith and the village leader. He misses his relatives when he's away on a Quest, and especially longs for Aunt Maria's famous cherry pie!

GOOD

92

50	AGE
100	POWER
35	MAGIC LEVEL
40	FRIGHT FACTOR
52	SIZE

MARLIK

THE DROWNING TERROR

Some say Marlik is like a man, but with tentacles around his neck and green scales over his skin. Others say that his form is liquid, and he lies like a pool of stagnant water, waiting to drown unfortunate swimmers.

AGE	258
POWER	232
MAGIC LEVEL	188
FRIGHT FACTOR	84
SIZE	120

MINOS
THE DEMON BULL

Minos was once a calm and gentle bull who grazed the fields of Seraph. When Malvel's minion Petra fed him magically poisoned seeds, this kind creature transformed into the Demon Bull. Cruel spikes jutted from his hooves and twisted horns sprouted from his head and nose. They were sharp enough to tear a person to shreds.

94

GOOD

27	AGE
273	POWER
176	MAGIC LEVEL
97	FRIGHT FACTOR
295	SIZE

DANGER DESTINY

Minos blows
a foul-smelling
black steam out
of his nostrils.

MIRKA
THE ICE HORSE

This dreadful Beast is terrifying enough, with his clawed hooves and sharp blue teeth. But even staying well back won't keep you safe – the Ice Horse's long tail is capable of shooting a hail of sharp shards with every whip and lash!

96

DANGER DESTINY

Mirka is a terrifying combination of fire and ice.

97

EVIL

AGE	386
POWER	249
MAGIC LEVEL	188
FRIGHT FACTOR	90
SIZE	157

MORTAXE

THE SKELETON WARRIOR

Mortaxe resides in the Gallery of Tombs. In life, he was three times the height of a normal man, and the casket he lies in is one of the largest there. Although Mortaxe was once a brave warrior, he was turned to evil and held the power to control all the Good Beasts of Avantia.

358	AGE
280	POWER
180	MAGIC LEVEL
90	FRIGHT FACTOR
145	SIZE

DANGER DESTINY

The Gallery of Tombs is found down a long staircase lit with crystals.

MURK
THE SWAMP MAN

The Swamp Man lurks in the boggy Kayonian marshlands. Murk's body is made of mud and decaying plants, and his scalp bristles with flame. He waits beneath the surface of the dark waters, snatching any poor creature unfortunate enough to become stuck in the algae-filled sludge. Soon, only their bones remain.

DANGER DESTINY

Murk's power is reduced on dry land, away from the mud of the swamp.

M

EVIL

101

AGE	271
POWER	212
MAGIC LEVEL	181
FRIGHT FACTOR	87
SIZE	241

MURO
THE RAT MONSTER

With a body five times the size of a bull, the Rat Monster rampages through the fields of Kayonia. On dark nights, you might catch a glimpse of his yellow eyes gleaming between the cornstalks, or hear his horrible whistling squeak. His pink tail whips back and forth and his whiskers are as sharp as blades.

EVIL

300	AGE
243	POWER
156	MAGIC LEVEL
82	FRIGHT FACTOR
230	SIZE

DANGER DESTINY

Tom defeated Muro by chopping off his tail!

NANOOK
THE SNOW MONSTER

104

GOOD

One of Avantia's Good Beasts, Nanook's shaggy fur keeps her warm on the Icy Plains. She has piercing eyes and curved claws. The pounding of her massive feet can crack ice, though this loyal Beast does her best to protect this part of the kingdom.

105

DANGER ✦ DESTINY

Nanook's bell forms part of Tom's shield and protects him from the cold.

AGE	335
POWER	165
MAGIC LEVEL	131
FRIGHT FACTOR	73
SIZE	265

NARGA

THE SEA MONSTER

This multi-headed sea Beast can terrify attackers into thinking they are dealing with several separate creatures. Its many eyes glow with fury, yellow and orange against its scaly skin. The stench of this Beast has been known to make grown men pass out in a dead faint.

106

EVIL

346	AGE
233	POWER
146	MAGIC LEVEL
87	FRIGHT FACTOR
310	SIZE

107

Tom uses Narga's jewel to give him perfect memory.

DANGER DESTINY

NIXA
THE DEATH BRINGER

Many people do not know they have crossed paths with Nixa until it is too late, for the Beast can adopt any disguise that she wishes. This is how she lures the nomads of the Dead Valley to their deaths. Nixa may be terrifying, but she does have a weakness: she cannot bear to look at her own hideous true form.

108

DANGER · DESTINY

Nixa disguised herself as Elenna to trick Tom.

109

EVIL

AGE 259
POWER 208
MAGIC LEVEL 176
FRIGHT FACTOR 90
SIZE 160

NOCTILA
THE DEATH OWL

326 AGE
210 POWER
145 MAGIC LEVEL
 79 FRIGHT FACTOR
121 SIZE

Elenna helped Tom to lure Noctila into a massive net.

This Beast is like a giant owl, with burning orange eyes. His grey feathers drip with thick black tar that can burn a person's skin from their flesh. His beak opens to reveal jagged teeth as he sends out screeches that can deafen anyone nearby. His talons are deadly weapons and the gleam of evil can be seen in the black slits of his eyes.

111

EVIL

OKAWA
THE RIVER BEAST

EVIL

52 AGE
295 POWER
193 MAGIC LEVEL
97 FRIGHT FACTOR
110 SIZE

This mysterious monster was created by magic which infected a normal person, slowly transforming them into a Beast. Okawa is stronger than several men. His flesh is slimy sinew, and his back is protected by a hardened shell of green scales. Worst of all, his poisoned touch is enough to make you lose your mind, turning his victims into mindless slaves.

Okawa has only one weakness. If the hollow in the top of his skull goes dry, he loses his power. So keep him away from water, and you might stand a chance!

113

DANGER DESTINY

An evil spell transformed Tom's uncle Henry into Okawa!

PLEXOR

THE RAGING REPTILE

Fishing communities in the kingdom of Tangala tell scary stories about the legendary "Cursed Fish", whose capture brought rains to help farmers. But no one actually believes the story, even though they hold an annual festival in which they capture a model version of the creature. They should not be so careless – for beneath the waters lurks Plexor, a monstrous reptile whose gaping mouth can swallow whole boats...and unlucky fisherfolk!

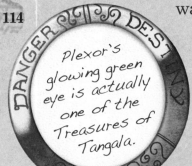

DANGER DESTINY

Plexor's glowing green eye is actually one of the Treasures of Tangala.

253	AGE
195	POWER
201	MAGIC LEVEL
85	FRIGHT FACTOR
291	SIZE

115

POLKAI

THE SHARK MAN

Before he was transformed into a Beast, Polkai was a man, the brother of Tom's enemy, Sanpao the Pirate King. Sanpao betrayed his brother, and cursed him to live his life as the Shark Man. Now, Polkai is one of the most terrifying Beasts in any kingdom – part man, part shark monster, he wields a poison-tipped cutlass that is even more deadly than his rows of jagged, vicious teeth.

116

DANGER DESTINY

The fin on Polkai's head is his only weak spot.

35	AGE
187	POWER
100	MAGIC LEVEL
83	FRIGHT FACTOR
102	SIZE

EVIL

QUAGOS

THE ARMOURED BEETLE

One of the four ancient Beasts of Tangala, Quagos is a giant armoured beetle with the strength to burrow through the hardest earth and smash down walls. Her gleaming shell can withstand most blades, and her iridescent spikes can puncture flesh with ease. While the silver sceptre of Tangala is safe, Quagos cannot harm the kingdom.

302	AGE
294	POWER
179	MAGIC LEVEL
91	FRIGHT FACTOR
289	SIZE

EVIL

DANGER DESTINY

The silver sceptre protects Tangala against evil Beasts.

RAFFKOR
THE STAMPEDING BULL

Raffkor, like the other young Beasts cared for by Wilfred the Beast-Keeper, grew up in the safety of Rion. He was a Good Beast, until he was turned evil by one of Kensa's wicked enchantments. Raffkor's mighty horns produce a magical blue fire that makes him a fearsome opponent.

120

DANGER ♦ DESTINY

Tom returned Raffkor to goodness by cutting off his blackened horn.

R

121

GOOD

AGE 4
POWER 223
MAGIC LEVEL 181
FRIGHT FACTOR 85
SIZE 262

RAKSHA
THE MIRROR DEMON

Raksha is not really one Beast, but several. He can only be summoned into the world under a strict set of conditions. First, it must be the height of summer, and second, he comes only from the Lake of Light, a hidden pool lying between the Forest of Fear and the Central Plains of Avantia. An enchanted Mirror lures other Good Beasts of Avantia to the Lake's edge, where Raksha can draw upon their combined powers.

122

257	AGE
292	POWER
200	MAGIC LEVEL
98	FRIGHT FACTOR
310	SIZE

EVIL

DANGER DESTINY

Raksha's armour is incredibly strong.

RASHOUK

THE CAVE TROLL

Rashouk lurks in the caves of the Dead Peaks, one of the most terrifying parts of the Forbidden Land. He is five times as wide as a man, and his powerful body makes him very dangerous. Rashouk does have one weakness – if a warrior can lure him into the open, he will have a chance to exploit Rashouk's fear of bright light. Sunshine, fire, lightning – all can be used as weapons against the Cave Troll.

321	AGE
165	POWER
154	MAGIC LEVEL
81	FRIGHT FACTOR
300	SIZE

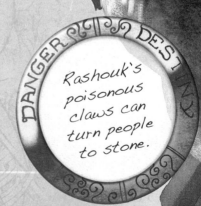

DANGER DESTINY

Rashouk's poisonous claws can turn people to stone.

125

EVIL

RAVIRA

RULER OF THE UNDERWORLD

Ravira rules the Underworld of Avantia. She lives in a castle made of glistening white stone, high above a city and surrounded by rivers of molten lava. She is guarded by the Hounds of Avantia, which can tear a person to shreds.

126

359	AGE
291	POWER
190	MAGIC LEVEL
91	FRIGHT FACTOR
98	SIZE

REPTUS

THE OCEAN KING

Little is known of this mysterious Beast, except that his body dwarfs most ships. Unscrupulous villains have tried to control him with a magical diamond which now lies at the bottom of the sea. All of Avantia prays that it stays there!

GOOD

AGE	311
POWER	177
MAGIC LEVEL	199
FRIGHT FACTOR	86
SIZE	304

R ROKK
THE WALKING MOUNTAIN

Rokk lives in the mountains surrounding the town of Tion, in Gwildor. He can hide easily among the boulder-strewn slopes, because he is actually made of rocks – boulders form his huge, squat legs and arms, and a great slab of stone makes his chest. Rokk's eyes are deep chasms that seem to suck in the light.

DANGER ⬥ DESTINY

Tom had to climb up into Rokk's eye sockets to defeat him!

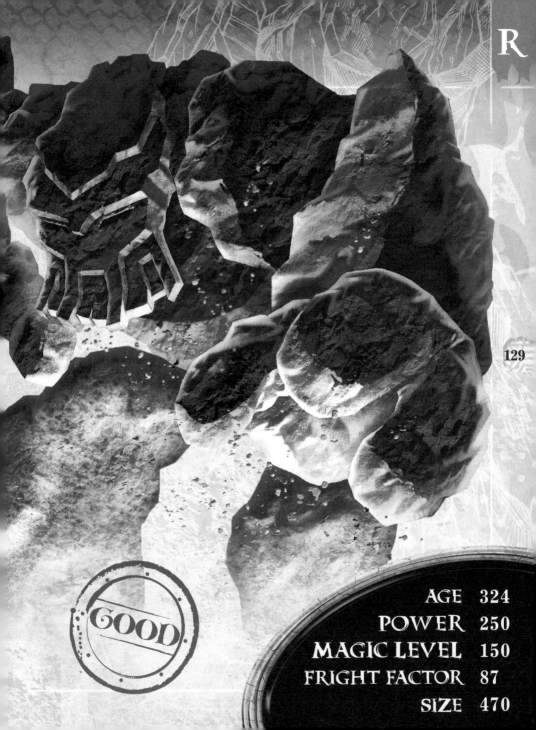

R

129

GOOD

AGE 324
POWER 250
MAGIC LEVEL 150
FRIGHT FACTOR 87
SIZE 470

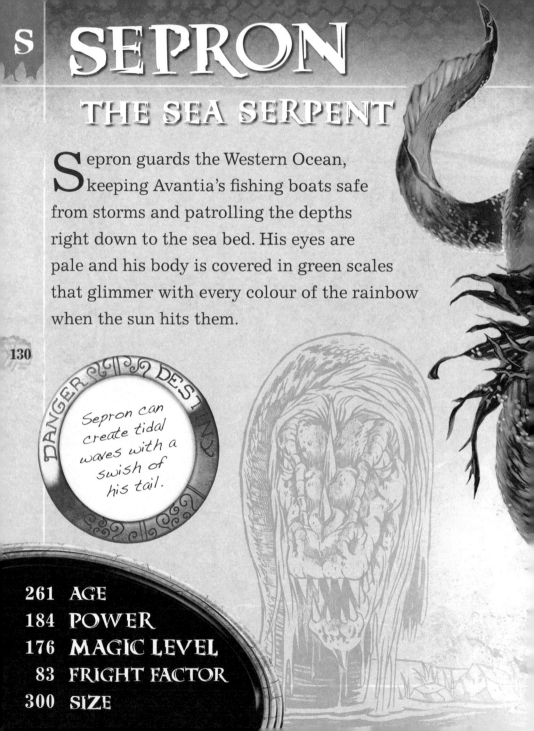

SEPRON

THE SEA SERPENT

Sepron guards the Western Ocean, keeping Avantia's fishing boats safe from storms and patrolling the depths right down to the sea bed. His eyes are pale and his body is covered in green scales that glimmer with every colour of the rainbow when the sun hits them.

130

DANGER — DESTINY

Sepron can create tidal waves with a swish of his tail.

261   AGE
184   POWER
176   MAGIC LEVEL
83   FRIGHT FACTOR
300   SIZE

GOOD

SERPIO
THE SLITHERING SHADOW

Serpio has the body of a giant snake, with scales that gleam in the darkness. He was created by the sorceress Kensa using the blood of Arcta the Mountain Giant, and like that Beast, he has only one eye, which glows brightly. He can breathe a hail of freezing water, encasing his victims in ice.

132

0	AGE
284	POWER
180	MAGIC LEVEL
87	FRIGHT FACTOR
327	SIZE

EVIL

DANGER DESTINY

Tom fought Serpio in a dark old mineshaft.

SHAMANI

THE RAGING FLAME

Shamani takes the form of a huge cat, with black fur that gleams like spilt oil. He can leap twenty paces in a single bound and he has long, vicious fangs. Shamani is an ancient Beast, once defeated by the Red Knight of Forton. This Beast's roars are so loud they splinter rocks, and sparks fly when he rakes his claws across the ground. With a flick of his tail, he can knock a grown man flying.

EVIL

330 AGE
220 POWER
155 MAGIC LEVEL
82 FRIGHT FACTOR
192 SIZE

134

S

DANGER DESTINY

Shamani's claws are made of magical amber.

SILVER

GOOD

When Elenna was a young girl, she injured herself in the woods and was rescued by a grey wolf, who let her sit on his back as he carried her home. She would go on to name the wolf Silver, and he has walked loyally by her side ever since.

35	AGE
147	POWER
34	MAGIC LEVEL
60	FRIGHT FACTOR
35	SIZE

SILVER
THE WILD TERROR

In the land of Seraph, the evil wizard Malvel used the Warlock's Staff to turn Silver into a terrifying Beast many times his usual size.

GOOD

137

AGE	35
POWER	270
MAGIC LEVEL	150
FRIGHT FACTOR	95
SIZE	237

S

SKOLO

THE BLADED MONSTER

If it had not been for Avantia's ruler, King Hugo, being infected with the rare, deadly Skolodine poison, Tom would not have had to venture into the Darkmaw Caves in search of an antidote – and it is possible that this giant, steel-winged centipede Beast would have remained unseen in her lair for many, many years.

138

GOOD

DANGER DES

Skolo uses a sticky purple goo to trap her victims.

392	AGE
285	POWER
183	MAGIC LEVEL
94	FRIGHT FACTOR
297	SIZE

139

SKOR

THE WINGED STALLION

Fear this creature! His long, yellowish teeth can tear chunks of human flesh, because they drip with acidic saliva. Silver sparks flash from his eyes and his wingtips scatter golden light. Don't be distracted by the shimmering colours, however – this Beast does not bleed, so he is unstoppable in battle. Even the deadliest blow will not wound Skor!

EVIL

DANGER · DESTINY

Skor is a fearsome enemy both on land and in the air.

AGE	264
POWER	221
MAGIC LEVEL	132
FRIGHT FACTOR	78
SIZE	160

SKURIK
THE FOREST DEMON

The repulsive, foul-smelling Forest Demon is one of the most frightening Beasts found along the Warrior's Road. This giant maggot-like creature steals children and traps his victims alive in sticky sacs hung from the trees in the woods near Tom's home village, Errinel.

EVIL

142

367 AGE
196 POWER
137 MAGIC LEVEL
 91 FRIGHT FACTOR
304 SIZE

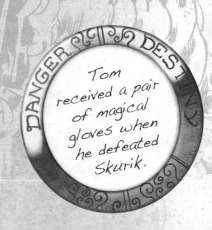

DANGER DESTINY

Tom received a pair of magical gloves when he defeated Skurik.

S

SLIVKA

THE COLD-HEARTED CURSE

Slivka dwells in the jungle, sliding between trees and shooting from the undergrowth in a flash. This giant lizard's muscular body is covered in blue scales. His tail can smash down trees, and his wide head is crested with jutting horns. Slivka can rise up on two rear legs, slashing with his claws, or whip out his long tongue to snatch his victims and draw them towards his sharp teeth.

DANGER ✧ DESTINY

Tom and Elenna battled Slivka on the Warrior's Road.

EVIL

S

145

AGE 371
POWER 245
MAGIC LEVEL 130
FRIGHT FACTOR 90
SIZE 289

SOLAK

SCOURGE OF THE SEA

Solak is a giant shark-like Beast, feared by even the bravest sailors. His sleek silvery body seems to change colour as he slides through the water, offering camouflage – first glowing blue, then indigo, then grey. His eyes stare with cold hatred upon his victims. He has several rows of teeth in his gaping mouth, trailing scraps of torn flesh, and his many fins are made of serrated bone.

EVIL

146

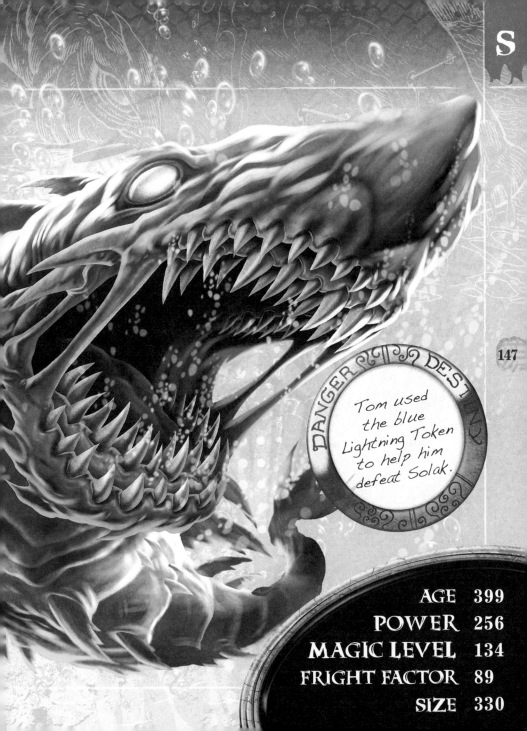

147

DANGER DESTINY

Tom used the blue Lightning Token to help him defeat Solak.

AGE	399
POWER	256
MAGIC LEVEL	134
FRIGHT FACTOR	89
SIZE	330

SOLTRA

THE STONE CHARMER

Soltra stalks the misty marshes near Tom's village of Errinel. Her face glows milk-white like the full moon. Soltra appears beautiful and draws you nearer with her charms. But be careful! If you stare into her one eye for too long, your body will turn to stone…

148

- 487 AGE
- 196 POWER
- 184 MAGIC LEVEL
- 72 FRIGHT FACTOR
- 107 SIZE

EVIL

SPIKEFIN

THE WATER KING

Brenner, an innocent fisherman, was slashed by Malvel with a poisoned blade and drowned in the sea. He re-emerged as Spikefin: half man, half sea-creature. Spikefin's ferocious claws, razor-sharp fins and huge whipping tail can destroy any boat sailing in his path.

149

GOOD

AGE	39
POWER	250
MAGIC LEVEL	180
FRIGHT FACTOR	85
SIZE	220

SPIROS
THE GHOST PHOENIX

Spiros is no ordinary phoenix. She is known as the lost Seventh Beast of Avantia. The evil wizard Malvel bewitched Spiros, separating her body from her soul, and now she lives between life and death. She is rarely seen in the skies over the kingdom, and no ordinary person can tame her.

GOOD

376	AGE
250	POWER
189	MAGIC LEVEL
89	FRIGHT FACTOR
235	SIZE

151

DANGER · DESTINY

Spiros has the
rare power of
All-Sight.

STEALTH
THE GHOST PANTHER

All the known kingdoms dread Stealth. He has a panther's lithe grace, and three tails that he can use to snatch up his enemies, tossing them into his mouth like morsels of food. Even a warrior who escaped those tails would be at the mercy of his deadly teeth and giant claws.

EVIL

153

DANGER???DESINY

One scratch from Stealth's claws can turn his victims evil!

AGE	243
POWER	199
MAGIC LEVEL	150
FRIGHT FACTOR	89
SIZE	155

STING

THE SCORPION MAN

S ting was created by the evil wizard Malvel. The Beast lived in the terrifying, dark tunnels beneath Malvel's Gorgonian castle. Tom and Elenna were attacked by Sting's giant pincers in a crumbling chamber, from which they only just managed to escape!

15	AGE
248	POWER
162	MAGIC LEVEL
71	FRIGHT FACTOR
100	SIZE

STORM

GOOD

S

Storm was born in King Hugo's stables, and at first he was nervous and jumpy. Fortunately, the wizard Aduro realised that Storm had an important role to play in Avantia's future and that Tom was his true master. Storm can gallop long distances without tiring.

155

AGE	15
POWER	200
MAGIC LEVEL	89
FRIGHT FACTOR	50
SIZE	60

TAGUS

THE HORSE-MAN

GOOD

Tagus the Horse-Man patrols the Central Plains of Avantia, guarding cattle from hyenas and wolves. He has the torso of a man, but the body of a powerful stallion. Though small compared to the other Good Beasts of Avantia, he towers over normal men and can gallop faster than any horse.

156

406	AGE
73	POWER
114	MAGIC LEVEL
58	FRIGHT FACTOR
100	SIZE

TALADON

Tom's father, Taladon, was once a boy knight who set off on a Quest of his own to discover more about Avantia's Beasts. A brave warrior, he became Master of the Beasts. Now Taladon's Golden Armour has been passed on to his son, Tom, the new Master of the Beasts.

157

GOOD

AGE	48
POWER	201
MAGIC LEVEL	176
FRIGHT FACTOR	80
SIZE	55

TARGRO

THE ARCTIC MENACE

Targro prowls the icy wasteland, his pale lilac fur helping him blend in with the snow. Sniffing the air with a pointed snout, he searches for any traveller foolish enough to be lost in the snow. If you're lucky, you might hear the creak of his clawed feet dipping in and out of the drifts, but more likely the first and last thing you'll know is the stink of his rotting breath.

370	AGE
232	POWER
134	MAGIC LEVEL
89	FRIGHT FACTOR
268	SIZE

EVIL

T

DANGER · DESTINY

Tom used one of Targro's claws to help defeat Slivka.

TARROK
THE BLOOD SPIKE

EVIL

160

A dreadful Beast created by the witch Kensa, Tarrok brings fear to the desert in the west of Henkrall, flinging a hideous yellow sap that encases his victims in a ghastly cocoon. His muscular body is covered with cruel red spikes that can repel even the bravest of warriors.

DANGER DESTINY

Tarrok is like a monstrous cactus with his spines and sap.

AGE	0
POWER	287
MAGIC LEVEL	150
FRIGHT FACTOR	89
SIZE	268

TAURON

THE POUNDING FURY

This horrifying "buffalo-man" was created by Kensa the Witch from the blood of Tagus, Avantia's Horse-Man. Tauron is terrifying enough with his vicious hooves and deadly horns – but his creator Kensa has also armed him with a lethal two-pronged blade that can slice a man in half!

162

0	AGE
296	POWER
155	MAGIC LEVEL
88	FRIGHT FACTOR
281	SIZE

EVIL

163

DANGER DESTINY

Tauron is a master swordsman.

TECTON

THE ARMOURED GIANT

Tecton is an ancient Beast, once defeated by the White Knight of Forton. With four powerful legs, his body is covered in a thick hide of overlapping armour plates bristling with spikes. His short legs don't stop him from moving quickly – Tecton has a different method of chasing his prey. He can curl into a ball like a giant hedgehog and roll across the ground to crush his victims.

DANGER DESTINY

Tom defeated Tecton using an icicle-shaped diamond.

164

EVIL

T

AGE 323
POWER 208
MAGIC LEVEL 132
FRIGHT FACTOR 78
SIZE 304

TERRA

CURSE OF THE FOREST

The people of Kayonia have long told stories of a monstrous tree with the power to move through the forest: this is Terra. The Beast is covered in bark and moss, like a tree trunk. Indeed, he looks so much like a tree that many don't realise the danger they face until it's too late. When he attacks, his terrifying eyes emerge from beneath the bark and he reveals teeth like vicious splinters. He uses his branches to squeeze the life out of his victims.

EVIL

312	AGE
263	POWER
168	MAGIC LEVEL
72	FRIGHT FACTOR
260	SIZE

GER DESTI

Terra turned
animals and
people alike
into wood.

TIKRON

THE JUNGLE MASTER

GOOD

168

Tikron is a Good Beast but was put under a wicked spell by Kensa.

After laying eyes on this giant monkey Beast for the first time, an adventurer might try to back away to a "safe" distance – but that won't stop Tikron from bursting eardrums with his deafening screech. With his whip-like tail and terrible claws, Tikron is a ferocious opponent at both long and short range.

AGE	6
POWER	239
MAGIC LEVEL	156
FRIGHT FACTOR	87
SIZE	210

TOM

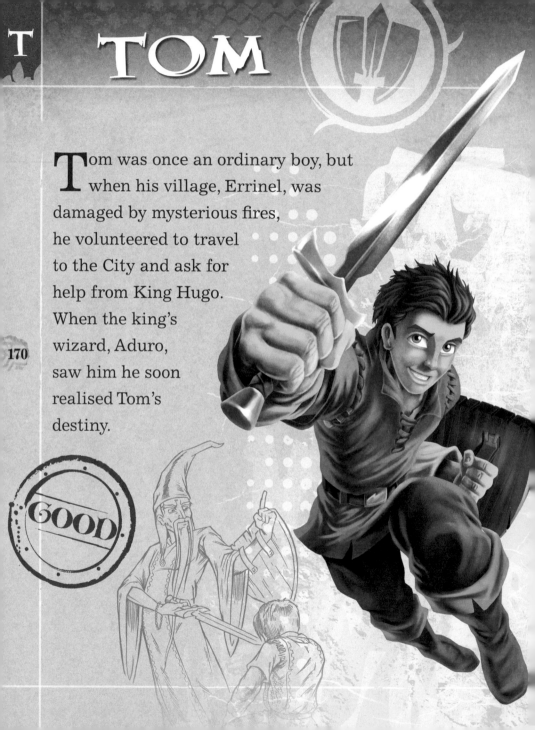

Tom was once an ordinary boy, but when his village, Errinel, was damaged by mysterious fires, he volunteered to travel to the City and ask for help from King Hugo. When the king's wizard, Aduro, saw him he soon realised Tom's destiny.

GOOD

As long as there is blood in his veins, Tom will continue his Beast Quests and do his best to protect the Kingdom of Avantia and all the known realms. Tom is armed with a sword given to him by Aduro, and his shield contains powerful tokens from the Good Beasts of Avantia.

171

Tom is the bravest boy in Avantia!

AGE	12
POWER	89
MAGIC LEVEL	132
FRIGHT FACTOR	74
SIZE	40

TORGOR

THE MINOTAUR

Torgor's thick, glistening coat of coal-black hair makes him almost impossible to spot in the night, though moonlight will pick out the two twisted horns that rise from his head. These horns are the key to Torgor's strength – removing them is the only way of defeating him...if you can get past his axe!

EVIL

224 AGE
210 POWER
126 MAGIC LEVEL
 74 FRIGHT FACTOR
144 SIZE

DANGER ~ DESTINY

Tom now wears Torgor's belt, which contains six jewels with magical powers.

TORNO
THE HURRICANE DRAGON

The violent winds that blow through the Northern Mountains are caused by Torno, one of the Beasts controlled by Sanpao the Pirate King. The Hurricane Dragon's foul breath is enough to blast his enemies through the air!

256 AGE
267 POWER
181 MAGIC LEVEL
91 FRIGHT FACTOR
291 SIZE

EVIL

T

175

DANGER DESTINY

Sanpao once controlled Beasts using magic from the Tree of Being.

TORPIX

THE TWISTING SERPENT

Torpix lives in the northwest of Seraph, among the dangerous mountains. He is the guardian of the Eternal Flame. His body is as long and thick as an oak tree, and his green and yellow scales are stronger than iron and covered with nasty spikes. His forked tongue can hurl yellow acid that melts through wood and metal.

DANGER DESTINY

Torpix sneaks up on his victims and squeezes the air from their bodies.

176

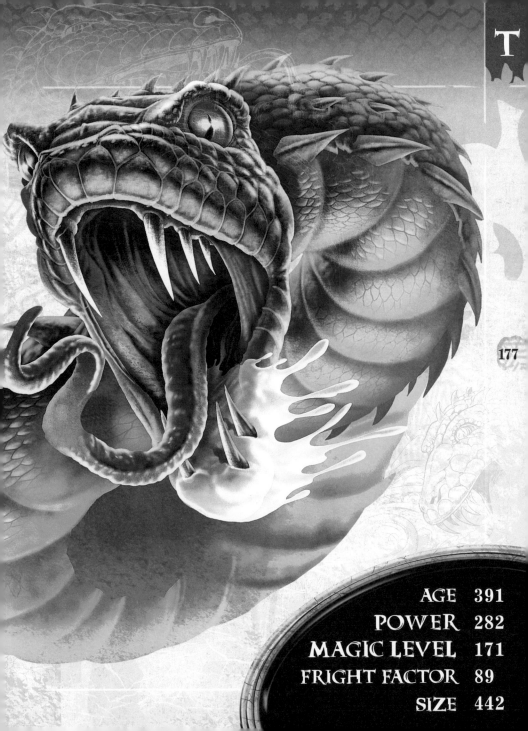

177

AGE 391
POWER 282
MAGIC LEVEL 171
FRIGHT FACTOR 89
SIZE 442

TREMA
THE EARTH LORD

GOOD

Trema tunnels through the earth, using his sharp claws and jagged teeth to defeat enemies. His muscular body is covered in thick blue armour tough enough to withstand the strongest sword blows. His glowing red eyes help him see in the darkness and a row of jewels sparkles across his forehead.

406	AGE
178	POWER
178	MAGIC LEVEL
95	FRIGHT FACTOR
306	SIZE

TRILLION

THE THREE-HEADED LION

Trillion is armed with one tail for balance when jumping and running, three brains to plan his attack and four paws for movement and fighting. With claws that can slice through rocks and ninety teeth that can shatter bones, this is a mighty opponent!

EVIL

AGE	303
POWER	202
MAGIC LEVEL	193
FRIGHT FACTOR	85
SIZE	115

TUSK

THE MIGHTY MAMMOTH

Tusk's brown, shaggy hide covers a body taller than the tallest tree. This Beast bellows and roars with anger, so you know immediately when she is going to attack. Her victims can try to run for cover, but her trunk will ripple out like a snake to crush them. A drop of the slime from the Beast's golden tusks will send poison racing through their body and death is almost inevitable.

EVIL

180

DANGER DESTINY

Tusk's enormous feet can squash her victims.

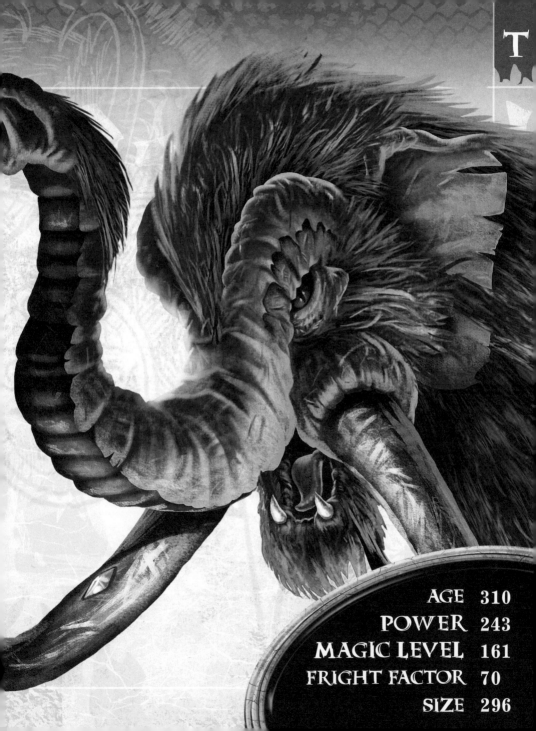

T

AGE 310
POWER 243
MAGIC LEVEL 161
FRIGHT FACTOR 70
SIZE 296

URSUS
THE CLAWED ROAR

Like the other Beasts of Seraph, Ursus was not always so fearsome and brutal. He was once a gentle bear who protected the inhabitants of the forest, but he was turned evil by Malvel's cruel magic. This Beast terrifies his enemies with his deafening roar, dagger-like teeth and colossal claws.

172 AGE
271 POWER
179 MAGIC LEVEL
90 FRIGHT FACTOR
300 SIZE

DANGER DESIGN

Ursus can smell the fear of his prey.

VEDRA AND KRIMON
TWIN BEASTS OF AVANTIA

New Beasts of Avantia are born very rarely. Vedra and Krimon are twin baby dragons who share a special bond. They hatched from the same egg, which had lain hidden for centuries in the Nidrem Caves.

184

VEDRA

0	AGE
150	POWER
126	MAGIC LEVEL
50	FRIGHT FACTOR
120	SIZE

Because they are Good Beasts, they cannot attack – they can only protect. This meant that they were vulnerable to Malvel, the Dark Wizard.

DANGER DESTI

Tom and Elenna rescued the dragons with help from Ferno and Epos.

185

GOOD

KRIMON

AGE	0
POWER	131
MAGIC LEVEL	146
FRIGHT FACTOR	50
SIZE	120

V

VERMOK
THE SPITEFUL SCAVENGER

EVIL

377	AGE
253	POWER
138	MAGIC LEVEL
95	FRIGHT FACTOR
167	SIZE

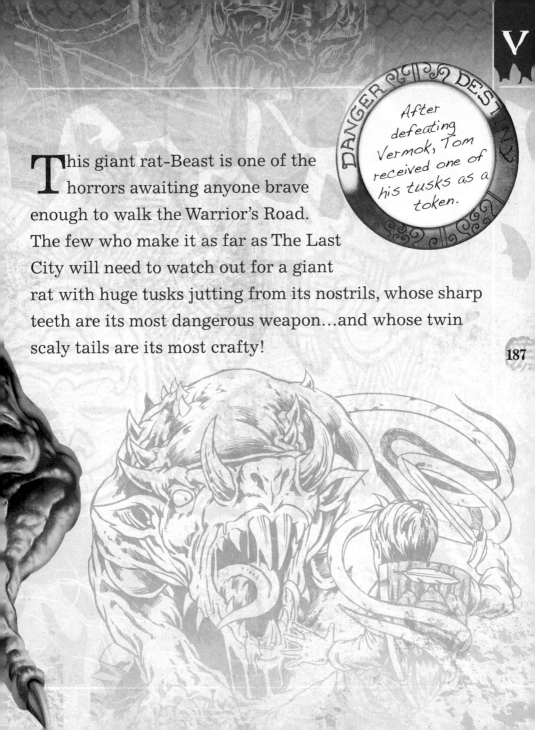

This giant rat-Beast is one of the horrors awaiting anyone brave enough to walk the Warrior's Road. The few who make it as far as The Last City will need to watch out for a giant rat with huge tusks jutting from its nostrils, whose sharp teeth are its most dangerous weapon...and whose twin scaly tails are its most crafty!

DANGER DESTINY

After defeating Vermok, Tom received one of his tusks as a token.

187

VESPICK

THE WASP QUEEN

Vespick's armour-plated body is twice as tall as a man's and her wings give her terrifying speed and agility. She is armed with six brutal hooked claws and a stinger which oozes a deadly green venom. One drop will instantly kill her prey. Worst of all, Vespick has an army of wasps at her command. They swarm around her victims, weakening them with excruciating stings.

285	AGE
253	POWER
173	MAGIC LEVEL
83	FRIGHT FACTOR
127	SIZE

EVIL

DANGER DEST

Poison from
a wasp sting
was used in a
potion to revive
Freya.

VIGRASH

THE CLAWED EAGLE

400	AGE
258	POWER
130	MAGIC LEVEL
88	FRIGHT FACTOR
252	SIZE

EVIL

V

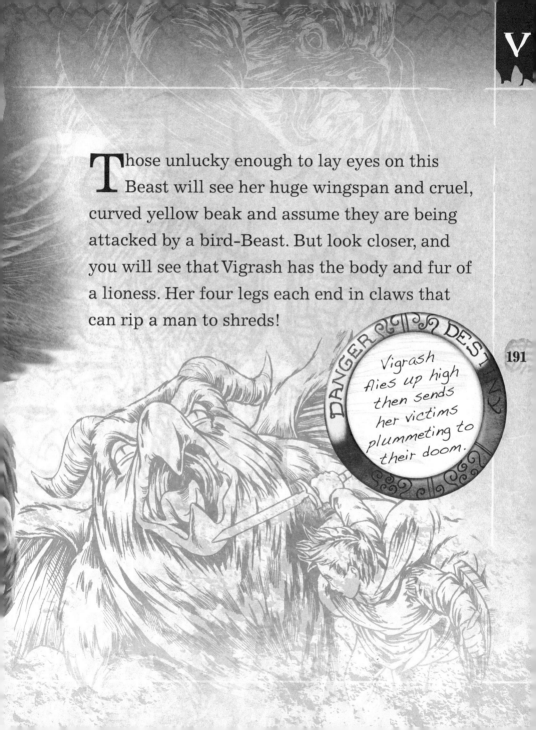

Those unlucky enough to lay eyes on this Beast will see her huge wingspan and cruel, curved yellow beak and assume they are being attacked by a bird-Beast. But look closer, and you will see that Vigrash has the body and fur of a lioness. Her four legs each end in claws that can rip a man to shreds!

DANGER DESTINY

Vigrash flies up high then sends her victims plummeting to their doom.

VIKTOR
THE DEADLY ARCHER

Viktor is the last of the Deadly Archers, cruel hunters who stalked the kingdoms looking for Beasts to kill. His bow shoots golden arrows with the power to suck the life-force from his victims, leaving them as mindless husks. The Deadly Archer is ten feet tall, with a horned helmet and a sharp, heavy broadsword.

EVIL

421	AGE
293	POWER
154	MAGIC LEVEL
96	FRIGHT FACTOR
137	SIZE

193

DANGER DESTINY

Viktor's skeleton horse is called Ossator.

VIPERO
THE SNAKE MAN

Anyone who survives the long journey into the depths of Avantia's blisteringly hot Ruby Desert might have the misfortune of crossing paths with Vipero. He is one of the largest reptiles in any of the known kingdoms. His two vicious snake-heads contain fangs that drip with poison. Most interesting is the human torso in the middle of his long, green body, which gives him the ability to reach out and grab his enemies.

194

DANGER DES

With two heads, Vipero is a fearsome opponent. Which one will strike?

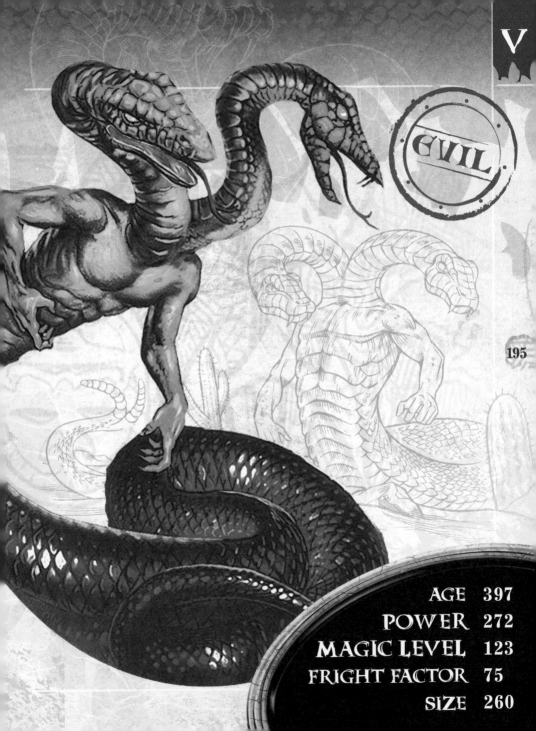

V

EVIL

195

AGE 397
POWER 272
MAGIC LEVEL 123
FRIGHT FACTOR 75
SIZE 260

VISLAK

THE SLITHERING SERPENT

Vislak can slither silently across the ground, or rear up as tall as a tree to tower over his foes. Spines crest his broad head and back. Some say he can taste fear with his flickering black forked tongue. Once he's pinned you with his stare, venom squirts from his razor-sharp fangs. But it isn't poison. Once the venom hits his prey, it hardens into a resin from which there's no escape.

5	AGE
231	POWER
159	MAGIC LEVEL
88	FRIGHT FACTOR
278	SIZE

GOOD

V

DANGER DESTINY

Vislak has the power to control other snakes.

VOLTREX
THE TWO-HEADED OCTOPUS

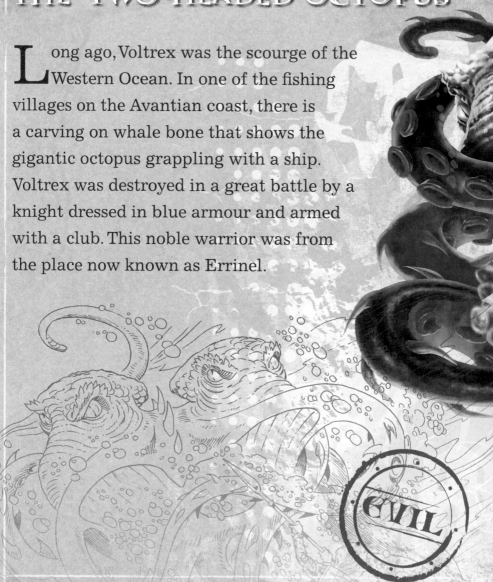

Long ago, Voltrex was the scourge of the Western Ocean. In one of the fishing villages on the Avantian coast, there is a carving on whale bone that shows the gigantic octopus grappling with a ship. Voltrex was destroyed in a great battle by a knight dressed in blue armour and armed with a club. This noble warrior was from the place now known as Errinel.

EVIL

V

DANGER DESTINY

Voltrex can crush rocks with his powerful beak.

AGE 325
POWER 253
MAGIC LEVEL 164
FRIGHT FACTOR 80
SIZE 269

W WARDOK
THE SKY TERROR

S ome say Wardok, an ancient Beast of Tangala, is a dragon. He has a sinuous body covered in purple scales, and leathery wings. He can swoop and fly with the agility of an eagle. The Beast's claws, like curved cutlasses, can snatch up cattle, or people, with ease. For the people of Tangala, the Beast's howl echoing through the hills was a signal to run indoors and hide.

EVIL

211 AGE
261 POWER
152 MAGIC LEVEL
88 FRIGHT FACTOR
281 SIZE

W

The precious Crown of Tangala was caught on one of Wardok's talons.

DANGER · DESTINY

XERIK
THE BONE CRUNCHER

In the paddy fields of south-western Tangala lurks Xerik, a horrifying plant-Beast who rises up from the boggy earth to snap his monstrous jaws. The Beast's tendril-roots can snatch up victims from even great distances. Tom had to venture into the Beast's jaws to retrieve the Ring of Tangala, which was concealed deep in Xerik's putrid mouth.

202

DANGER DESTINY

Xerik has eyes inside his mouth so he can see his victims!

X

203

AGE 320
POWER 235
MAGIC LEVEL 149
FRIGHT FACTOR 94
SIZE 322

EVIL

YAKORIX

THE ICE BEAR

For a long time, the myths said, Yakorix slept beneath the ice of Avantia's arctic north, but when awoken she was as deadly as ever. She is a great bear, towering taller than a house, with spikes jutting from her spine and glowing eyes that narrow in on her victims. Her huge paws are powerful enough to crush a person, making the ground shake as she charges across the snow. The only way to conquer Yakorix is to bury her under the ice once again.

315	AGE
232	POWER
147	MAGIC LEVEL
91	FRIGHT FACTOR
290	SIZE

Y

The Good Beast Nanook faces terrible danger when Yakorix rises again...

DANGER ∙ DESTINY

ZEPHA
THE MONSTER SQUID

The powerful tentacles of Zepha the Monster Squid churn the waters of the Western Ocean, creating whirlpools and even changing the direction of the currents. The people of the fishing villages went hungry because the Monster Squid had scared away so many fish. Luckily Tom and Elenna were able to defeat the Beast.

DANGER DESTINY

Zepha can blind his victims using his squid ink.